SURYA

VISHWAKARMA, THE COSMIC ARCHITECT, HAD A DAUGHTER CALLED SANJNA.

THE CHILD PLAYED ALL DAY IN THE HOT SUN.

SURYA'S RAYS HARDLY SEEM TO AFFECT HER.

SHE CAME INTO THE HOUSE ONLY WHEN THE SUN HAD SET.

SURYA SEEMS TO FASCINATE HER.

I HAVE OBSERVED THAT.

AS SANJNA GREW UP, HER LOVE FOR THE SPLENDOUR OF THE SUN INCREASED.

I ENVY YOU. YOU WILL HAVE SURYA'S WARMTH ALL YOUR LIFE.

AS FOR ME, I SHALL HAVE TO GET MARRIED SOON AND...

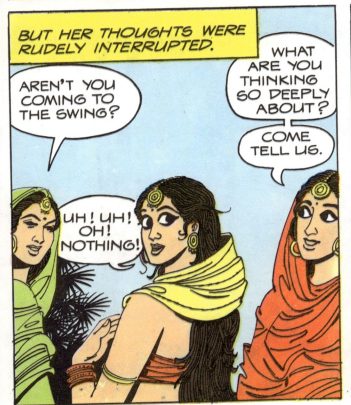

BUT HER THOUGHTS WERE RUDELY INTERRUPTED.

AREN'T YOU COMING TO THE SWING?

WHAT ARE YOU THINKING SO DEEPLY ABOUT?

COME TELL US.

UH! UH! OH! NOTHING!

I WAS WONDERING HOW LONG I WOULD BE ABLE TO REVEL IN SURYA'S WARMTH.

3

AS LONG AS THERE ARE SWINGS IN THE GARDEN!

LATER—

LET US GO IN. IT IS ALMOST DARK AND I AM TIRED.

THE NEXT DAY VISHWAKARMA TOOK HIS DAUGHTER OUT ON AN ELEPHANT RIDE.

SANJNA, YOU ARE NO LONGER A LITTLE GIRL...

I KNOW, FATHER...

FATHER! LOOK! SURYA THE MOST GLORIOUS OF THE CELESTIALS!

WOULD YOU LIKE TO HAVE SURYA FOR YOUR HUSBAND?

FATHER!

VISHWAKARMA APPROACHED SURYA WITH HIS DAUGHTER.

I SHALL BE ONLY TOO GLAD TO WED YOUR FAIR DAUGHTER.

BUT WHAT DOES SANJNA SAY?

MY FATHER HAS SPOKEN MY WILL.

VISHWAKARMA DREW SANJNA ASIDE.

THINK WELL. ARE YOU SURE YOU WILL BE ABLE TO BEAR HIS BRILLIANCE IN ALL SEASONS?

I AM SURE, FATHER.

WHERE IS MOTHER?

SHE AWAITS YOU.

I SEEK YOUR BLESSINGS, MOTHER.

MAY YOU EVER BE HAPPY.

THE DAY OF THE WEDDING SOON DAWNED. AS THE BRIDE WAS BEING ADORNED—

LET ME DARKEN YOUR EYES. YOU WILL NEED PROTECTION FROM HIS GLANCES.

GLARE, YOU MEAN.

NEED PROTECTION FROM SURYA'S GLANCES! ME?

THE WEDDING TOOK PLACE WITH GREAT POMP.

7

AFTER THE WEDDING SURYA TOOK SANJNA TO HIS ABODE IN THE SKIES.

SANJNA LOVED HER NEW HOME AND WAS VERY HAPPY.

SOON A SON WAS BORN TO THEM. THEY CALLED HIM MANU.

THE CELESTIAL SAGES CAME TO BLESS THE BABY.

HE SHALL BE THE WISEST AMONG THE WISE.

MANU GREW UP AS PREDICTED.

SURYA AND SANJNA WERE PROUD OF HIM.

HE IS BRILLIANT!

LIKE HIS FATHER!

THEN SUDDENLY ONE SUMMER...

...SURYA'S RAYS BEAT DOWN...

...INTENSE AND OPPRESSIVE.

HE WAS AT HIS ZENITH.

COME, SANJNA, SIT BY ME.

SANJNA! LOOK AT ME! I AM YOUR HUSBAND!

SANJNA! WILL YOU REPEL ME?

I AM SORRY, MY LORD!

THEN LISTEN CAREFULLY. SINCE YOU CLOSED YOUR EYES ON ME, THE SUSTAINER OF ALL LIVING BEINGS, THE SON YOU BEAR NOW, SHALL BE YAMA, THE GOD OF DEATH.

BUT SURYA VANISHED AND SANJNA WAS LEFT ENVELOPED IN DARKNESS.

THE MONTHS PASSED BUT SANJNA DID NOT DARE GO TO SURYA.

THEN AS DECREED BY SURYA, YAMA THE TERRIBLE...

...AND YAMUNA THE INCONSTANT WERE BORN TO SANJNA.

BLAMELESS ONE, YOU TREMBLE AS YOUR HAPLESS MOTHER DID!

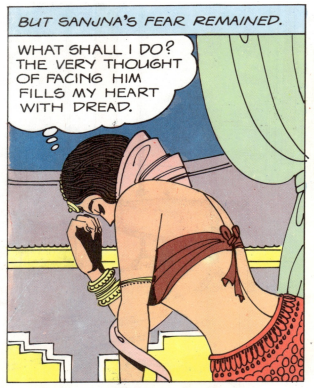

BUT SANJNA'S FEAR REMAINED.

WHAT SHALL I DO? THE VERY THOUGHT OF FACING HIM FILLS MY HEART WITH DREAD.

I MUST FLEE. AWAY...AWAY FROM HIM!

BUT WHO WILL CARE FOR MY LORD? AND MY CHILDREN? AH, THERE LIES CHHAYA, MY SHADOW.

SO SANUNA LEFT FOR HER PARENT'S HOME.

WHEN FATHER INSISTS THAT I RETURN TO MY HUSBAND, I WILL GO INTO THE FOREST.

VISHWAKARMA THOUGHT THAT HIS DAUGHTER HAD COME ON A VISIT.

WELCOME MY DAUGHTER. IS ALL WELL WITH YOU?

NO, FATHER! YOU WERE RIGHT. I COULD NOT BEAR THE BRILLIANCE OF SURYA IN SUMMER.

SANUNA SPENT A FEW HAPPY DAYS THERE.

THEN ONE DAY—

SANJNA, YOU HAVE PLEASED ME BY YOUR VISIT. BUT...

...IT IS NOT PROPER FOR A MARRIED GIRL TO STAY IN HER PARENTS' HOME FOR TOO LONG.

GO NOW TO YOUR HUSBAND. BUT COME AGAIN TO SEE ME.

I DOTE ON YOU. BUT A WOMAN'S PLACE IS BY HER HUSBAND.

AS I HAD FORESEEN.

SO SANJNA LEFT HER PARENTS' HOME AND WENT INTO THE FOREST.

I CANNOT FACE SURYA. I WILL TURN MYSELF INTO A MARE. THEN NO ONE WILL FIND ME.

NOW I SHALL DO PENANCE TO REDUCE THE STRENGTH OF SURYA'S GLARE.

MEANWHILE CHHAYA HAD REACHED SURYA'S ABODE AND HAD TAKEN SANJNA'S PLACE.

MY LORD, FORGIVE ME. I HAVE OVERCOME MY WEAKNESS.

YOU HAVE COME BACK TO ME!

23

SANJNA, I HAVE FORGIVEN ALL LONG AGO.

MY LORD! IF ONLY I HAD KNOWN.

SO THESE ARE HER CHILDREN.

CHHAYA WAS HAPPY IN HER NEW HOME.

POOR SANJNA HAD TO GIVE UP ALL THIS. WILL SHE EVER RETURN?

CHHAYA SOON HAD A SON.

I MUST NOT FORGET THAT I AM ONLY SANJNA'S SHADOW.

THEN ANOTHER SON AND A DAUGHTER WERE BORN TO HER.

SANJNA WILL NOT RETURN.

CHHAYA LOVED HER CHILDREN AND SPENT MOST OF HER TIME CARING FOR THEM.

BUT ALAS! SHE DID NOT CARE FOR SANJNA'S CHILDREN IN THE SAME MANNER.

GET AWAY FROM MY SIGHT, YOU ACCURSED CHILDREN.

COME, MY DEAR ONE. LET US GO TO YOUR FATHER.

MANU FORGAVE HER FOR THIS BUT YAMA COULD NOT.

THERE SHE IS! NOW CRUEL TO YAMUNA. MOTHER, WHAT HAVE WE DONE TO DESERVE THIS?

HOW I WISH I WERE MOTHERLESS.

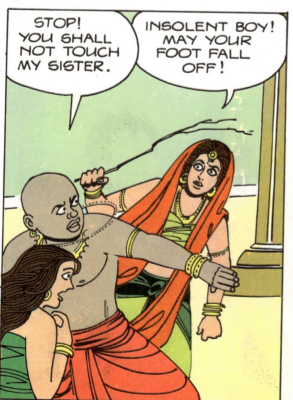

STOP! YOU SHALL NOT TOUCH MY SISTER.

INSOLENT BOY! MAY YOUR FOOT FALL OFF!

YAMA DECIDED TO SPEAK OUT TO HIS FATHER. AFTER HE HAD FINISHED —

FATHER, THAT WOMAN IS NOT OUR MOTHER!

I AGREE. A SON MAY CHANGE IN HIS AFFECTIONS BUT A MOTHER NEVER CEASES TO CARE.

SHE DID NOT WANT TO LEAVE YOU UNCARED FOR. SO SHE SENT ME HERE INSTEAD.

WHERE IS SHE NOW?

WITH HER FATHER.

WHERE IS SANJNA?

SURYA WENT TO SEE VISHWAKARMA.

SHE CAME HERE SEEKING REFUGE FROM YOUR BRILLIANCE.

WHERE IS SHE NOW?

I HAVE DIVINED THAT SHE TURNED HERSELF INTO A MARE.

SHE WANDERS IN THE FOREST DOING PENANCE TO OBTAIN A MILDER FORM FOR YOU.

THEN REDUCE MY BRILLIANCE AND LET US GO TO HER.

VISHWAKARMA REDUCED SURYA'S BRILLIANCE BY CHISELLING AWAY AN EIGHTH OF HIS RAYS. THEN THEY WENT IN SEARCH OF SANJNA.

HAVE YOU SEEN A MARE GO BY?

YES! A QUAINT ONE... BY THE RIVER.

WHY DO YOU CALL IT A QUAINT ONE?

I SPEAK THE TRUTH, SIR. THIS MARE TALKS!

IT MUST BE SANJNA.

SURYA WENT UP TO THE MARE.

SANJNA! I AM SURYA, YOUR HUSBAND. PLEASE TAKE YOUR OWN FORM.

NOT UNTIL I HAVE OBTAINED THE BOON I SEEK.

THE BOON YOU SEEK IS ALREADY YOURS.

I HAVE CHISELLED AWAY AN EIGHTH OF HIS BRILLIANCE.

SANJNA TOOK HER OWN FORM.

FATHER! DEAR FATHER!

MY LORD! HOW ARE OUR CHILDREN?

MANU, YAMA AND YAMUNA WILL KNOW A MOTHER AGAIN.

I SHALL NEVER AGAIN WANDER AWAY FROM HOME.

CHHAYA SHALL BE FORGIVEN AND SHALL LIVE WITH US.

GO, MY CHILDREN. MAY YOU LIVE FOREVER IN PEACE.

SO SURYA AND SANJNA WENT BACK TO HIS ABODE IN THE SKIES AND LIVED THERE IN HAPPINESS WITH CHHAYA AND THE CHILDREN.

DIAL-A-COMIC

To buy any Amar Chitra Katha or Tinkle Comic

Call Toll Free on 1800-233-9125 (Mon-Fri 9.30 am to 6.00 pm IST or leave a voice mail)

or

SMS 'ACK BUY' to 575758 and we will call you back

or

Log on to www.amarchitrakatha.com to select your favourite comics and read story-of-the-week online

TINKLE
WHERE LEARNING MEETS FUN